The City Of Ice

Tami Jenkins

The City Of Ice

Jade had been counting down the days until she went on holiday; she was so excited because her Daddy had told her they were going to the City of Ice. She had even marked her calendar and had been counting down the days.

The little dragon had gotten up early, so she could finish packing her cases ready for the long journey. This year she wasn't just going with her parents; she was also going with her friend, which made it all the more exciting; because they could do all sorts together.

There was a knock on the door; Jade shouted down from her bedroom,

"I'll get it"

She ran down the stairs, almost tripping as she went; to let her friend Fern in.

As she opened the door she quickly said

"Come in; come in" adding

"Are you as excited as I am?"

Fern nodded her head and said

"I have been looking forward to this for a long time"

Fern wasn't a dragon like Jade; she was a little fox that lived in the forest of wonder.

As they stood talking Jade heard her Mummy calling from the kitchen;

"Come and sit down; your breakfast is ready"

They both skipped into the kitchen just as two bowls of steaming dragon oats were placed in front of them.

"This smells yummy" Jade said
Fern was quick to agree.
"Tuck in before it gets cold" Fern said; adding
"Then we can go and look for your sledge to take
with us"
Smiling at each other; they began to eat their
breakfast, it soon turned into a race to see who
would finish first.
Jade placed her spoon into the bowl and was quick
to shout
"I am the winner, I finished before you Fern"
The little fox wasn't far behind her friend and
placed her spoon down to.
Jade looked over to her Mummy,
"Can we go and look for the sledge to take with us
please?" she asked.
"Yes; but don't be too long; we have to go soon"
she replied smiling at her daughter.
They both left the table and scampered outside to
her Daddy's shed; after a few moments of searching
they had found what they were looking for.
Jade giggled and said to Fern that now they had
found it; they could go sledging down some of the
steepest hills and have so much fun.
They returned back to the house to find Jade's
Daddy waiting and ready to go.
He was stood by the door; with all the magic bags
packed.
She looked up at him and said

"Can we take the sledge with us?"
He nodded and smiled saying he was sure he could find room in with everything else.
Jade and Fern climbed onto his back and they started to make their way across the Kingdom of Fantasy and Make Believe.
They were watching the clouds pass them by and listened to the birds singing and chattering away in the trees.
"It all looks so pretty in the morning" Fern said
Jade nodded her head and agreed.
As they passed over the Forest of Wonder, they saw Lightening playing in the morning sunshine; chasing butterfly fairies.
Jade called out "Hello down there"
Lightening looked skywards and shouted
"Have a nice time; I will see you when you come back"
He waved to them until they disappeared from sight.
Jade asked her Daddy how long it would take them to get there; he smiled and said
"Be patient my darling we will be there soon; I promise"

Both of the girls were sleepy, they had been so excited the night before that neither of them had slept much. They both snuggled up to each other and slowly drifted off to sleep; dreaming of all the adventures they would have.

Her Daddy had told her of all the times he had been there when he was a young dragon; and all the good times he had.

Jade's Mummy flew silently through the sky; saying very little, but just smiling as she went.

The dragons had been flying for quite some time, when they both woke up feeling very cold.
The weather had started to change; it didn't take long for them both to realize that the ground below them was covered in snow and ice.
Jade smiled broadly
"We are there" she said excitedly
"Where" Fern asked; wiping the sleep from her eyes.
"The City of Ice; silly" answered Jade.
Both were really excited by now, Jade pulled on her Daddy's tail
"Please can we land now? PLEASE" they both said together.
This time her Mummy spoke
"Be patient you little Imps"
But the tone she said it in was as always with love.
It wasn't much longer before they finally landed and started looking for a cave to spend their holiday in.
Both of them jumped down and to their surprise they began slipping and sliding everywhere.
Jade wasn't on her feet long; before she landed on her bottom. She asked her Daddy if they could take the sledge while he searched for a cave to stay in.
"You can have your sledge; as long as you promise not to go too far" he replied.
Together they both said "We promise"

Moments later they were going in search of some hills to use it on. Fern was sat down and Jade was pulling her along; they were talking away to each other, both laughing at how Jade had landed on her bottom when they landed.

"It's alright for you Fern; you have four legs I only have two" Jade mumbled.

They both found the perfect hill just a short way from where they were and together they pulled the sledge behind them and climbed.

As they had gotten a little further up they could hear someone else laughing and playing.

"I wonder who that is" Jade said

"I don't know; let's go and look" Fern replied.

They soon saw a baby Polar bear playing with a seal pup.

"Hello" Jade said "We are on holiday"

They both looked up from where they were playing
and the Polar Bear spoke
"We live here, what are your names" he asked
Jade introduced herself,
"My name is Jade and this is my friend Fern" she
said.
"My name is Snowflake" replied the polar bear,
"I am Sally" said the Seal.

Jade was curious about what they were doing and she just had to ask

"What are you doing?"

"We are building a Snowman" Snowflake replied

"Would you like to help" He then asked.

"Yes please that would be fun" Fern replied very quickly

Building a snowman was fun, but building with their new found friends even more so.

Jade and Fern were both curious what the carrot was for, so this time Fern asked

"Why have you got a carrot?"

Sally told her that it was for the nose on the snowman.

Jade's paws were starting to get very cold after rolling the snow into a giant ball.

"Would you both like to play on our sledge?" she asked looking towards Sally

Well neither Sally nor Snowflake had ever been on a sledge before and for Sally it seemed a little scary, but Snowflake was always brave and adventurous.

"I have never been on a sledge before Jade" said Sally

The polar bear was quick to say it looked like fun.

All four of them started to climb the rest of the way to the top of the hill; once at the top; Jade said for them all to hop on and hold tight and she would push them down.

Once they were all seated, she gave a huge push and the sledge started to slide from the top and make its way downhill.

There were shrieks of delight coming from Snowflake and Fern, but Sally was scared as she held on tightly to her friend.

"It's Okay" shouted Snowflake

By the time they were close to the bottom, Sally had started to enjoy the ride.

Jade was still at the top, jumping up and down with excitement, already she was having so much fun.

Once at the bottom, they all called up to their friend

"We are coming back up"

They dragged the sledge behind them and quickly made it back to the top

"It is your turn now Jade" Fern said

She sat herself down and held on tight as the other three pushed as hard as they could.

Snowflake had the idea of sliding down on his tummy and was soon followed by Sally and Fern.

"The last one to the bottom is a loser" Shouted Snowflake as he whizzed past her at a fast pace.

Well Jade didn't want to lose, so she twitched her magic nose and made herself go faster than she had ever gone before; but what she hadn't seen was the very large pile of snow at the bottom; by the time she had seen it; it was too late and she went head first into the drift; disappearing right into the middle of it.

Snowflake had tried to warn her, but she hadn't heard his calls. The friends ran over to the snow pile and started to dig Jade out of it, laughing as they were throwing snow in every direction.

A small voice could be heard

"I won the race"
At this point they knew Jade was safe and unharmed; they sighed a sigh of relief.
The little dragon had learnt a lesson and promised that she would never cheat again.
Like most small children, they soon grew bored, jade wondered out loud if there was anywhere exciting they could all go.
The others scratched their heads for a few moments and then Sally said
"I know where we can go"
Snowflake quickly reminded his friend that they had to go home now.
"Meet us back here tomorrow and I will take you to meet Eli the Eskimo." She said.
"We will be waiting here by the snowman" Fern said.
"Ok see you all in the morning" called Sally as she started to walk away.
On the walk back to jade's parents; the excited pair spoke of their new friends; and how much fun they were having on their first day.
As they approached the caves they had passed earlier they could hear voices,
"That's my Daddy talking" Jade said
"I think they must be in there" she said again pointing in the direction of the cave.
They walked in to find that everything had been set up; ready for them to go to sleep that night.

The two youngsters started talking about their day and new friends; when her Mummy stopped her and said
"There will be plenty of time to tell us about your day darling; we have someone we would like you to meet"
"Who?" she asked
Her Daddy turned to his daughter and said
"This is Eli; he is an Eskimo and lives in an igloo"
Jade smiled and softly said hello
"We were coming to see you tomorrow; our friends were going to bring us to your house"
Eli gave off a loud laugh
"Let me guess who your friends are; they must be Snowflake and Sally, am I right?" he asked
Jade was amazed at how Eli could possibly know this,
"How did you know" she asked
Eli started to explain that he had found Snowflake as a tiny cub; all alone with nobody to love him, so decided to take him home.
"Why was he on his own" Jade asked
"Well…" said Eli Pausing a while
"He was an orphan"

Fern looked very confused unsure what an orphan was,
"What is an orphan?" she asked shyly
Eli looked at the little fox and began to explain, that Snowflake didn't have a Mummy or Daddy like she and Jade had, so he decided that he would take him home and care for him; like their parents do for them.

Jade felt very sorry for Snowflake and she had tears
falling down her cheek
"How very sad, poor Snowflake" she said between
sobs
"What about Sally?" said Fern?
"Sally had swam too far from her parents and had
got lost" he said
"I found her sat on a loose piece of ice in the middle
of the water; crying for her Mummy, so just like
Snowflake she came to live with me"
Jade was rubbing her tired eyes and yawning,
"Well I will leave you in peace, it has been a long
day for you all" Eli said as he stood up.
They all said Goodbye to the Eskimo as he left the
cave,
"See you tomorrow" Jade called out.
The smell of Berry soup was drifting around the
cave; they were all very hungry and so they sat
down to eat; before going to bed.
Once finished, the two friends sat back yawning and
stretching;
"Mummy I am tired" Jade said
Fern was almost asleep standing up, so they were
shown to their beds,
Slowly pulling back the covers the two children
climbed into the soft warm blankets; they chatted
for a while and then fell fast asleep, dreaming
wonderful dreams of their day full of adventure

Early the next morning they were both wide awake,
Jade decided she would go and jump on her Daddy
to wake him up
"Daddy, Daddy wake up" she yelled at the top of
her voice
Opening one eye and looking at his daughter he
said
"It is far too early, go back to bed Jade"
Of course he knew that neither of them would go
back to sleep; they were clearly too excited.
Finally Jade's Mummy got up out of bed and made
them their breakfast, this morning they had Magic
berry crunch.
Fern was the first one to finish and proudly
announced herself the winner;
"I won, I won" she said with a cheeky grin.
"Well done" said Jade
After everyone had finished they asked if they could
go out and find their friends.
"Yes" came the reply
It was a relief for them all; as the youngsters had
not given them a moment's peace since they woke
up.
Fern said to Jade that they could run up to the
snowman and see if they could see Sally and
Snowflake from there.
Once at the snowman they decided after the count
of three they would call out for their friends
"ONE; TWO, THREE" counted Jade

"Sally, Snowflake where are you?" they called together, it echoed across the hill and down into the valley.
There was no reply, so they called again and listened carefully.
They could hear in the distance Snowflake saying "Hurry up sally our friends are waiting"

By the time they had reached Fern and Jade; they were out of breath.
"We met Eli last night, he was at the cave with my Mummy and Daddy" Jade said
"We heard" said Sally
"Eli told us that he met you; he really likes you"
Fern was in a playful mood and she started to throw snowballs at everyone, one even landed right on top of Snowflakes head, everyone laughed at him.
Before they knew it, there were snowballs flying in every direction; they were having so much fun.
"Do you know of anywhere we can go and explore?" asked the little dragon
"We know lots of places; isn't that right Snowflake" Sally replied
"We do" he said
Fern had a mischievous look on her face and quickly said
"Let's go"
They started to walk across the snow looking for an adventure; wherever they could find it.
The polar bear had been telling them about a large cave he knew of, this one had large icicles hanging down from the ceiling and dripping down the walls. But these were no ordinary icicles; they were made completely of chocolate and candy, in all shapes and colours.

Jade had a very sweet tooth and loved candy; she was looking forward to getting there.

After a long trek they finally made it to the opening of the cave; they couldn't believe their eyes. Pink and white striped candy hung from the roof of the cave.

Snowflake had a warning for them before they walked in.

"There is a grumpy wolf that sleeps in this cave, he doesn't like it when others come in and take his candy" he said.

Neither Sally nor Snowflake had ever seen him, and they didn't really believe the story.

Jade was so tempted by the candy; that she couldn't resist snapping a small bit off to try.

Holding the bit she had broken off; she put it too her mouth, forgetting everything her friend had said.

There was no sign of the wolf, so they continued to eat whatever they could break off.

Fern had never seen so many different kinds of chocolate and sweets in one place.

Talking in a rather loud voice she said

"Ohhhh look at this, look at that"

Each of them had become a little louder and the greed was starting to show; they had completely forgotten about the wolf.

Suddenly there was a deep growling sound; coming from the back of the cave through the darkness.

"Oh my" said Sally

"That must be the wolf; I didn't think it was real"

She had truly believed it was a story Eli had made up.

All of a sudden, two red eyes came from the darkness, jade became frightened

"Quick we had better run; before he catches us" she said

The growl was getting closer and much louder, and then he spoke

"How dare you, what do you think you are doing in my cave?" he snapped.

They all ran towards the opening moving as fast as they could.

"And don't come back" the wolf shouted.

Jade and her friends had been running so fast that they hadn't noticed the wolf was no longer chasing them; they just ran and ran without looking back. Only when they stopped did they notice the wind was getting stronger and it was blowing the snow over their tracks.

They were lost; they didn't know how to get back, the sun was sinking

"It will soon be dark" said Jade.

The four friends were now very frightened and worried.
Snowflake thought may be Jade could use her magic nose to get them home again.
Jade thought this could work, so she twitched her nose; but nothing happened. After trying a few more times, but still nothing she said
"It is too cold for my magic to work"
"What are we going to do?" cried Fern
They continued walking, with no idea how they would find their way.
"May be we could find an igloo to sleep in" Sally said
But where were they going to find one of those, they were miles from anywhere. The sun had gone and the moon took its place, Jade knew her parents would be worried.
"I wish I hadn't been so greedy, and none of this would have happened" said Fern.
"It's my fault"
Jade was quick to reassure her friend
"Don't be silly Fern; we were all to blame; not just you"
She knew her Mummy and Daddy would be looking for them right now, because they had been gone a long time.
Jade was right, her parents and Eli were already searching for them, but they were worried too, because they didn't know where to look.

All snuggled up together the friends were doing
their best to keep warm, trying hard not to panic.
They began telling stories to each other to keep
their minds occupied.
Jade told them of her adventure in the Land of the
Lost Clowns, and how she had gone deep into the
ocean of tears to find Opal the clown.
Snowflake and the others were amazed at Jade's
bravery; and how wonderful it would have been if
they could have been there too.
The polar bear asked Jade if all the other clowns
were free to go back after the evil wizard had been
turned to stone.
"No sadly their shows had ended my friend, but
they were not sad, because life would once again
be happy and full of laughter. It was only the evil
wizard that made them so sad" she said.
The four friends started calling out for help
shouting
"Hello, is anybody there?"
Nobody could hear their cries or so they thought.
A strange looking bird waddled up beside them
"Are you lost?" he asked "May be I can help you"
"Hello" Jade said
"My name is Jade and this is Snowflake; Sally and
Fern" she said as she pointed towards her very cold
friends.
"Who are you" she asked still unsure

"I am Peewee the Penguin, you are lucky I heard
you; I was just on my way home"
Fern said quietly "I wish I was home"
Jade said to Peewee that her parents must be very
worried.
"Don't panic my little ones; you can come home
with me for the night. I would love to know how
you managed to get yourselves lost" the penguin
said.

The friends huddled together in a group and talked about whether they should go with the penguin or stay where they were.

Peewee said

"Snowflake you live with Eli, don't you?"

"Yes" replied the very confused polar bear

"How did you know that?" he asked.

"I know Eli very well; we go fishing together sometimes and he always talks about you and Sally" Peewee replied.

They agreed they would go with him, after all he did know Eli, they were sure they would be safe.

"But what about my Mummy and Daddy, they will be looking for me now?" Jade said.

"Don't fret I will get a message to them, letting them know you are safe and well" he replied.

All four of them agreed it would be safer than staying out in the cold all night.

When they arrived at Peewee's home there was a nice warm fire glowing and the smell of fish cooking; they were all happy to be in the warmth and Jade began to tell the penguin how they managed to get lost.

Jade continued to explain how they had stumbled across the cave that was covered in chocolate and candy icicles.

They had all become greedy, and in their excitement had made too much noise; which had woken up the wolf. He chased them out, growling and shouting at them.

They ran and ran, too scared to look back and before they realized it they were completely lost; the wind had been blowing and it had caused the snow to cover their footprints that had been left when they entered the cave.

"Once we knew we were lost, is when we started calling for help" she finished.

Peewee shook his head and then said

"You should have listened to the stories you were told about the wolf, shouldn't you?"

"Yes" they all answered with their heads hung in shame.

"We just thought it was a story that Eli had made up, we didn't think it was true, and for that we are very sorry" sally said.

Peewee told the friends he was going to get a message to Eli and Jade's mummy and Daddy; the he said

"You all sit here and stay warm and don't get into any more trouble while I am gone"

Jade promised that they would be good' so the penguin made his way out of the door.

Jade and her friends were watching him from the window as he went.

Whilst they were watching they saw Peewee look up into the sky and he called

"Magic star in the sky, please come down and I will tell you why"

The star was the brightest they had ever seen; they were all stood there in complete amazement, as it began to drift down and floated just above his head.

"How can I help you" said the star

Peewee explained that he had four friends in his house who were lost, he needed to get a message to Eli the Eskimo and to Jade's parents too.
The star gave a really big sparkle, and quicker than they could blink she had vanished into the night sky.
Once back indoors, Peewee assured them not to worry the message would get there very soon.
The star had started to make her way towards the large ice mountains and was flying high above them, all the time leaving a trail of magic stardust behind her.
She found the cave, and went inside to ask the wolf if he had seen Eli, bursting in like that had once again disturbed the wolf and he snapped
"What do you want?"
"You shouldn't be in my cave, you have no right"
The star just shook her head and said
"Stop with your temper you bad wolf; I just want to know if you have seen Eli today?"
"Why" snarled the wolf
"Because; you chased away four young friends today that meant you no harm, they were just children being adventurous, and now they are lost and their parents will be looking for them. I need to find them to tell them that the children are safe and well" she replied

"I am sorry, I didn't mean to frighten them that much, I really am a grumpy old wolf aren't I?" the wolf replied looking very sad and sorry for himself.
"Yes" replied the star "But you can help me look for Eli and the two dragons to make it up"
He was eager to help, he felt it was the least he could do after causing so much trouble.
They both headed towards the snowman that the friends had built on their first day in the city.
The wolf was struggling to keep up with the star "Slow down" he shouted "I can't keep up with you"

The star giggled as she dropped from the sky and asked the wolf if he was afraid of flying. The wolf didn't want to look like he was scared so in a deep voice he said
"Me? I am not afraid of anything, I am a brave wolf"
Smiling at him, the star sprinkled some star dust over his head and gently they drifted up into the sky.
It was clear to see he was frightened and so the star said
"I thought you weren't afraid of anything?"
Once he had become used to being in the air, he found himself enjoying it.
They were flying over the top of the mountains, when they saw Eli and the two dragons on the ground calling out for Jade and the others.
"That must be them" said the wolf
They started to gently drift down to where the three figures stood.
Eli looked up to the sky and waved to the star, once they were back on the ground; Eli asked them if they had seen Jade and her friends
"Yes, we have we were coming to look for you to let you know they are safe with Peewee" she said.
Jade's mum began to cry with happiness and said
"I am so glad they are safe, I thought they were lost forever; thank you"

The star told them to follow her bright light and it would lead them to where they needed to be.
Knowing they were all okay, the three took a gentle walk following the star dust in the sky.
The wolf and star had arrived at Peewee's house and gently tapped the door.
When the penguin answered, he jumped back at the sight of the wolf standing there.

"Don't be afraid of the wolf; he won't hurt you"
said the star.
"He helped me find Eli"
Although a little unsure, he invited them in to wait
for the others to arrive.
Jade and fern had fallen asleep listening to the
stories that Peewee was telling them, how he and
his friends would play on the frozen lakes.
Sally and snowflake were still wide awake and
quivering in the corner when they saw the wolf.
"I won't hurt you" he said "I am sorry I scared you,
it was very mean; please forgive me"
The wolf had just finished what he was saying when
Jade and Fern woke up
"I want my mummy" Jade cried out
"They will be here soon" replied Peewee.
The wolf told them they were all welcome to come
and visit him any time they liked, and promised he
would not chase them off again.
The four of them smiled and said they would come
and visit him soon.
It wasn't long before there was another knock on
the door and jade asked if she could answer it this
time; Peewee nodded his head and she ran to open
it.
Stood in front of her was her mummy, she threw
her arms around her so tight, Jade felt like she
would burst.

The star told everyone to look up in the sky on their way home and they would see something they had not seen before, being a curious dragon Jade asked what they would see.
The star replied "Just look into the sky, I will tell you no more"
Eli said it was time to head back, it was late and they were all tired, including him.
They all agreed and said thank you and goodbye to Peewee and the wolf.

Eli sat on Jade's mum's back and the four friends sat on her Dad's back, they were flying over the mountains and as they looked up into the sky, they couldn't believe their eyes.

The sky was alight with clouds of many colors, which zig zagged across the night; this was something Jade had never seen before.

"Wow; what is that" Jade asked Eli

"They are the northern lights, aren't they pretty?" he replied

She asked if she would see them again before she went back home.

"Probably if you look hard enough" he told her.

They all promised they would never stray that far from home ever again, they had learnt their lesson. Once back at the cave, Eli, Snowflake and Sally, all said goodnight and promised they would see each other again tomorrow.

After they had gone, Jade and Fern told them about their adventure and what they had seen; but they were so very tired, that they couldn't keep their eyes open any longer. They were tucked up in bed and wished a good night by Jade's parents.

The next morning Jade and Fern were up bright and early, they wanted to make the most of their last day together. They were soon joined by Sally, but Snowflake was still asleep, when she left to meet them.

They played on the sledge outside of the cave, keeping their promise that they would stay close to home; Jade's parents had joined in by the time Snowflake arrived and they were all being pulled along on the sledge.

This was the best holiday Jade had ever had and she knew there was so much to tell lightening about when she got back home.

The day slipped by so fast and she knew she would miss her new friends when they left tomorrow.

"Dad can Sally and Snowflake come and stay with us sometime in the kingdom of fantasy and make believe?" Jade asked

"Of course they can, and we can come back next year if you would like too" he replied

Jade jumped up and down excitedly, she was hoping they would come back again.

It was late once again and Eli took the little polar bear and seal back home, whilst Jade and Fern sat watching the Northern lights.

"It has been fun" Fern said

"Yes it has, I wish we didn't have to go home tomorrow" she replied

They both sat quietly for a while longer, and then went to bed; it would be a long journey home in the morning.

As the bags were almost packed Jade heard Sally in the distance

"Come on Snowflake, we will miss them if you are
not quick" she shouted.
Jade came out of the cave and waved to her
friends. They talked for a while, whilst everything
was being packed down, when they heard Jade's
Mummy calling
"It is time to go now" she said.
Jade and Fern hugged their friends tightly and
promised to keep in touch as often as possible.
Eli was waiting beside Jade's Daddy and gave them
both a big hug before they left.
"Be good and stay out of mischief" he said laughing.
They jumped onto her daddy's back and before
they knew it they were taking off, they waved until
their friends were out of sight.
The girls were talking and giggling at their big
adventures when Fern said
"I wonder if Lightening will come and see us today;
when we get back?"
"I am sure he won't be far away" Jade replied.
She wasn't wrong, because as soon as they landed,
she heard his hooves across the ground, he had
seen them flying in and was so excited to see his
friend.
"You must tell me everything about your holiday
and leave nothing out" he said

Jade knew there was so much to tell and they spent the rest of the day telling the little unicorn about the candy cave and the wolf; how they got lost and of course about their new friends too.
"I wish I had been there" he said smiling
"May be next year" Jade replied.
Eventually it was time for Lightening to return home and Fern too
"I will be back tomorrow, you can tell me more about it then" he said.
Although it was late and past Jade's bedtime; her Mummy had allowed her to stay up a little longer, so she could watch the northern star in the sky; knowing her little girl was still caught up in the magic of her holiday.
Jade yawned a big yawn and said
"Thank you for the best holiday that I have ever had"
Her mum and Dad smiled at their daughter and replied
"No Jade; thank you for being the best little dragon anyone could have and filling our hearts with so much love"
Jade drifted off to sleep, with images of her holiday in her mind and a sweet smile on her face.

The End

* 9 7 8 1 5 0 2 4 7 4 8 8 9 *